CROSS-COUNTRY SKIING

BY KARA L. LAUGHLIN

Published by The Child's World®
1980 Lookout Drive • Mankato, MN 56003-1705
800-599-READ • www.childsworld.com

ACKNOWLEDGMENTS
The Child's World®: Mary Swensen, Publishing Director
The Design Lab: Design
Heidi Hogg: Editing
Sarah M. Miller: Editing

PHOTO CREDITS
© alvant/Shutterstock.com: 14-15; Fotokvadrat/Shutterstock.
com: 10; Karen Faljyan/Shutterstock.com: 2-3; konstantinks/
Shutterstock.com: cover, 1; Levranii/Shutterstock.com: 4; l i g h
t p o e t/Shutterstock.com: 16; Olga Polyakova/Dreamstime.
com: 19; Sasha64f/Shutterstock.com: 12-13; Stephanie Murton/
Dreamstime.com: 20-21; Tomo Jesenicnik/Shutterstock.com: 6-7;
Val_th/Dreamstime.com: 9

ISBN: 9781503807723
LCCN: 2015958216

Printed in the United States of America
Mankato, MN
June, 2016
PA02300

TABLE OF CONTENTS

4

Time to Ski!

It is winter. Snow covers the ground. Bundle up! It is time to ski! Cross-country skiing (or **Nordic skiing**) is a bit like hiking on top of the snow.

Fast Fact!
Cross-country skiing is the oldest type of skiing.
It is at least 5,000 years old.

Equipment

Skiers use skis, boots, and poles. Cross-country skis are long and thin. They have a spot for boots called **bindings**. The bindings help the boots stay put.

Fast Fact!
Most skis today are made of fiberglass.

Three Ways to Ski

There are three ways to cross-country ski: **classic**, **skate**, and **backcountry**.

Classic skiing is slow and steady. It is a lot like walking. A skier bends forward and kicks back with one leg. That makes the other ski glide forward. Classic skiers keep their skis on the snow.

Skate skiers are fast! They look a lot like ice-skaters.

They push their feet out to the side. The skis come right out of the snow.

Tracks

Skiers use **groomed** tracks. A machine drives over the snow. It makes the snow hard and flat. At times a groomer leaves two tracks for skis to slide in.

Fast Fact!

Most classic skiers stay on the sides of groomed tracks. Skate skiers ski in the middle.

13

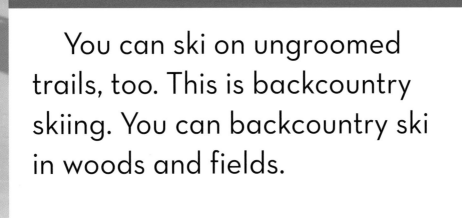

You can ski on ungroomed trails, too. This is backcountry skiing. You can backcountry ski in woods and fields.

Fast Fact!
"Ski touring" is a kind of backcountry skiing that lasts for several days.

Hills

To go up hills, make a V shape with your skis. This keeps you from sliding down the hill. This step is called the **herringbone**.

You can glide down a small hill. But what if a hill is steep? Then you need to hit the brakes! You can **snowplow** to slow down. This is when you point your ski tips slightly toward each other.

Fast Fact!
Be sure not to cross your ski tips.
If you do, you might fall.

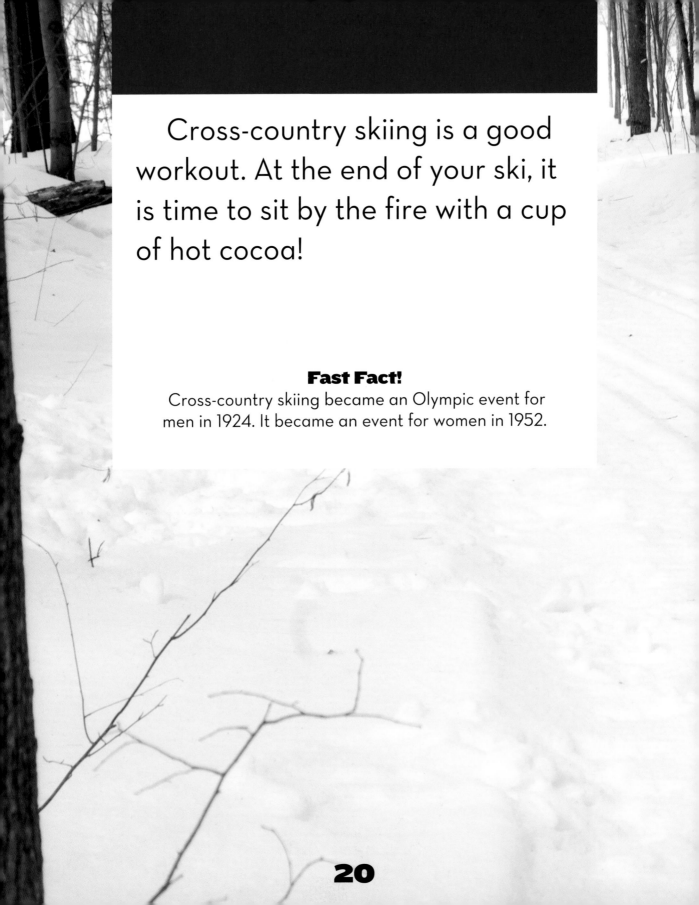

Cross-country skiing is a good workout. At the end of your ski, it is time to sit by the fire with a cup of hot cocoa!

Fast Fact!

Cross-country skiing became an Olympic event for men in 1924. It became an event for women in 1952.

Glossary

backcountry (BAK-kun-tree): A type of cross-country skiing done in places without groomed tracks is called backcountry skiing.

bindings (BYND-ings): Special tools that are attached to the ski. In cross-country skiing, they allow the boots to move up and down, but keep the toe clipped into the ski.

classic (CLAS-sik): The slow and steady way to cross-country ski. The skier kicks back with one leg while the other glides forward. It looks like walking on top of the snow.

groomed (GROOMD): Ski trails that have been made smooth and hard for skiers are groomed tracks.

herringbone (HAYR-ring-bohn): A way for skiers to go uphill, where the ski tips are pointed out to keep the skis from slipping back. It is named for the pattern the ski tracks make—like the spine of a fish.

Nordic skiing (NOR-dik SKEE-ing): Another name for cross-country skiing is Nordic skiing.

skate (SKAYT): A fast way to cross-country ski is called skate skiing. The skis are pushed out to the side and lifted up.

snowplow (SNOH-plow): A way that skiers slow down or stop. Skiers point the tips of their skis together to look like the top of an A. Then they push out while bending their knees.

To Learn More

In the Library

Burns, Kylie. *Biathlon, Cross-Country, Ski Jumping, and Nordic Combined*. New York, NY: Crabtree Publishing Company, 2010.

Van Dusen, Chris. *Learning to Ski with Mr. Magee*. San Francisco, CA: Chronicle Books, 2010.

On the Web

Visit our Web site for links about cross-country skiing:
childsworld.com/links

Note to Parents, Teachers, and Librarians: We routinely verify our Web links to make sure they are safe and active sites. So encourage your readers to check them out!

Index

About the Author

Kara L. Laughlin is an artist and writer who lives in Virginia with her husband, three kids, two guinea pigs, and a dog. She is the author of two dozen nonfiction books for kids.